Big Frank's Fire Truck

**A Random House
PICTUREBACK®**

Big Frank's

Dedicated to Orange County Fire Station #39: Ray Hutchinson, Bob Ouellette, Jim Boggs, Jim Hale, Stu Baker, Peter Beale, Ross Bergantine, Will Vellekoop, Bernie Brawner—L.M.

Special thanks to Hartley Field and the Mortlake Fire Department of Brooklyn, Conn.—J.M.

Fire Truck

By
Leslie McGuire

**Illustrated by
Joe Mathieu**

Random House 🏠 New York

Library of Congress Cataloging-in-Publication Data: McGuire, Leslie. Big Frank's Fire Truck / by Leslie McGuire ; illustrated by Joe Mathieu. p. cm. — (Random House pictureback) ISBN 0-679-85438-X 1. Fire extinction—Juvenile literature. 2. Fire fighters—Juvenile literature. [1. Fire extinction. 2. Fire fighters.] I. Mathieu, Joseph, ill. II. Title. III. Series. TH9148.M33 1995 628.9'25—dc20 94-1402

Manufactured in the United States of America   20   Random House, Inc. New York, Toronto, London, Sydney, Auckland

It's nine o'clock on Monday morning. Big Frank is just getting to work.

Big Frank is a firefighter. He works a twenty-four-hour shift. That means he will be on duty all day and all night.

This is the firehouse. This is where Big Frank lives, sleeps, and eats while he is at work.

Big Frank checks in and goes over his schedule. At eleven o'clock, he will make a fire inspection at the supermarket. At two o'clock, he will visit the elementary school to talk about fire safety.

Big Frank has to be prepared for all kinds of emergencies, too. Who knows what will happen during his shift!

office   kitchen

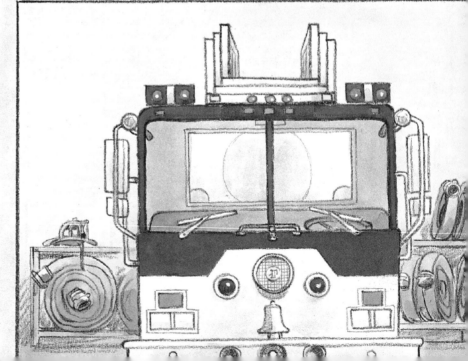

common room

bunk room

fire truck stalls

hook and ladder

The Fire Chief asks Big Frank to fuel up the fire trucks. Big Frank heads for the garage.

Big Frank's company has three fire trucks. The hook and ladder is used for aerial rescues. The brush breaker has four-wheel drive and can go where there are no roads. Big Frank drives the pumper engine. The pumper holds water—1,000 gallons!

brush breaker   pumper

After he takes care of the engines, Big Frank checks his gear.

He wears a helmet to protect his head, a fireproof coat and pants to protect his body, and sturdy boots to protect his feet. He has a wooden wedge for propping open doors, and an oxygen pack and mask in case the fires are very smoky.

Big Frank hangs his equipment next to the pumper engine. Now he is ready for anything.

Big Frank sits down with his partner Mike for a cup of coffee. Just then the fire bell rings. At the same time, the lights in front of the station start flashing, and the computer starts printing.

Accident at the intersection of Main Street and Laurel Road. Car on fire!

Mike, Janet, and Gary jump in the pumper with Big Frank. Big Frank turns on the siren and heads out of the station.

WHOO, WHOOOOOO!

The fire truck roars down Main Street with the siren going full blast. Cars pull over when they hear the noise, and a policeman waves the big engine right through a red light.

The firefighters arrive at the scene of the accident in less than four minutes.

The first thing Big Frank does is check to see if anyone is hurt. He is glad he has his paramedic training—one lady has a bad cut on her head. Big Frank bandages the cut, and Mike radios for an ambulance.

Meanwhile, Gary and Janet spray the burning car with a special foam made for gasoline fires. The flames go out, and a tow truck comes to haul the wrecked car away.

Big Frank returns to the station with the others and fills out his report. He looks at his watch—it's nearly eleven o'clock! He drives over to the KwikShop to make his inspection.

Big Frank inspects the store's sprinkler system to make sure it is working properly. He checks the emergency doors to see if they will open in case of a fire. He also runs a test of the alarm system. The supermarket has a smoke alarm that rings right in the fire station.

Everything looks okay.

EXIT

EMERGENCY ONLY

Back at the firehouse, Big Frank eats lunch with the other firefighters. Then he takes a short nap in his bunk.

At two o'clock, Big Frank and Mike drive the pumper engine over to Niceview Elementary School.

Big Frank and Mike talk to the second-grade class about fire safety. Mike tells them that smoke detectors are very important. He shows them how to check their smoke detectors at home.

Big Frank teaches the class what to do in case of a house fire. He tells them to stay low so they won't breathe too much smoke. Then he shows them how to Stop, Drop, and Roll!

On the way back to the station, a call comes in over the radio.

Brush fire at Derry Hill!

Big Frank turns the pumper around and heads for Derry Hill. He and Mike will meet the rest of the company there.

Big Frank is worried. There hasn't been any rain for a long time, and the wind is blowing. This could be a bad fire.

Big Frank and Mike reach the fire a little after four o'clock. They go right to work. They spray water around the edges of the blaze to keep it from spreading.

The wind blows, and sparks fly through the air. When the rest of the company arrives, the Fire Chief tells Janet and Gary to hose down the roofs of the nearby houses. That will help keep the sparks from setting the houses on fire.

At nightfall, the wind picks up speed. Suddenly, the
fire goes out of control and races toward the forest.

This fire is too big for one company
to handle alone. Big Frank radios for help.
Two more companies are on their way.

Big Frank knows all the firefighters in the other companies. He has worked with them many times. Together they make a good team.

By midnight, they have saved the nearby houses from catching fire. They have headed off the blaze to the north, south, and east. But the fire is still spreading west through the trees. Even the brush breakers can't keep up!

Big Frank calls in a squad of special firefighting helicopters. Soon they are whirring overhead.

The firefighters battle the blaze from the ground.
The helicopters drop chemicals from the air.
Finally, after fourteen hours, the fire begins to die out.
The worst is over.

Big Frank is tired. No wonder—it is nearly six o'clock in
the morning. As soon as the next shift of firefighters arrives,
Big Frank and his company head back to the firehouse.

Back at the station, Big Frank helps wash down the trucks. They are sooty from the fire.

Big Frank is dirty, too. He has ashes all over him—even in his hair. Big Frank jumps in the shower. Then he puts on clean clothes and eats a big breakfast.

It's nine o'clock on Tuesday morning. Big Frank's
shift is over.

Big Frank waves good-bye to the other firefighters.
He can't wait to go home. He can't wait to hug Amber
and Little Frank.

Big Frank will have two days off to spend with his family. Then he'll start another shift, fighting fires and helping everyone's family stay safe and sound.